D1329569

Mary Had a Little Jam
And Other Silly Rhymes

CREATED BY
BRUCE LANSKY

ILLUSTRATED BY
STEPHEN CARPENTER

Meadowbrook Press

Distributed by Simon & Schuster
New York

The Library of Congress has cataloged this title as the following:

Lansky, Bruce
The new adventures of Mother Goose: gentle rhymes for happy times / created by Bruce Lansky; illustrated by Stephen Carpenter.
    p.   cm.
Summary: A collection of contemporary Mother Goose rhymes, based on the original characters.
ISBN: 0-88166-201-1 (Meadowbrook) 0-671-87288-5 (Simon & Schuster)
    1. Mother Goose–Parodies, imitations, etc.   2. Children's poetry, American. [1. Nursery rhymes.   2. American poetry.]
I. Carpenter, Stephen, ill.   II. Title.
PS3562.A564N48   1993
811'.54–dc20

93-11129
CIP
AC

ISBN 0-88166-470-7 (Meadowbrook)
ISBN 0-689-03392-3 (Simon & Schuster)

©2004 by Meadowbrook Creations

Managing Editor: Elizabeth H. Weiss
Editorial Coordinator: Cathy Broberg
Production Manager: Kate Laing
Desktop Publishing Coordinator: Jon C. Wright
Designer: Tabor Harlow
Production Artist: Erik Broberg

Published by Meadowbrook Press, 5451 Smetana Drive, Minnetonka, MN 55343

BOOK TRADE DISTRIBUTION by Simon & Schuster, a division of Simon and Schuster, Inc., 1230 Avenue of the Americas, New York, NY 10020

07 06 05 04   10 9 8 7 6 5 4 3 2 1

Printed in Hong Kong

We would like to thank the teachers and students of the following kindergarten and preschool classrooms for taking time to help us select the poems for this collection. Your enthusiasm for this project has made it all the more worthwhile: Ann Adams, Blake School; Bessie Arne, Children's Workshop; Sally Budroot, Marlyce Erickson, and Kathy Pope, Groveland Elementary; Gene Ford, St. Margaret Mary Learning Center; Paige Frondell, Kids & Company; Richard Gosen, Wayzata Learning Center; Leah Grove, Turtle Lake Elementary; Dawn Hansen, Kids & Company; Irma Kelley, Orono Primary School; Cathy Kinee, Hope Daycare; Terry Laden, Hopkins Montessori; Jody Hlavka and Carol Wald, Kids' Art Studio; Tracey Orr, Peter Hobart School; Diane Schimelpfenig, Tanglen Elementary; Judy Spenser, Fulton Elementary; Linda Stewart, Deephaven Learning Center; Jana Rasmussen, St. David's Elementary; Jeanine Wanberg, Minnetonka Montessori; Nancy Burton Wiederhold, Deephaven Montessori; Eden Prairie Children's World; Eden Prairie KinderCare; Eden Prairie New Horizon Child Care; and Minnetonka Children's World.

Special thanks to the many parents and teachers who reviewed the manuscript, including: Jane Al-Tamimi, Polly Andersen, Kathryn Bartee, Jim and Bonnie Bohen, Ralph and Katie Dayton, Gary and Mary Elling, Mary Mackey Faulkner, Larry Holgerson, Marsha Jacobson, Doug and Catherine Kelley, Vicki McKinney, Kelsey Bush Nadear, Steve Sobieniak, Frank and Julie Stieve, Janice Surian, Linda Torres, Jon and Mary Wright, and many others.

CONTENTS

Old Mother Goose
 used to fly through the air,
riding a gander—
 they made a fine pair.

Now when she wants
 to get somewhere soon,
she rides on the cow
 that jumped over the moon.

Mary had a little jam;
   she spread it on a waffle.
And if she hadn't eaten ten,
   she wouldn't feel so awful.

Hickory, dickory, dock,
 a mouse jumped in my sock.
He wiggled his nose
 and tickled my toes,
which gave me quite a shock!

Hickory, dockory, hic,
 the day your clock gets sick,
and says, "Tock Tick,"
 but not, "Tick Tock,"
call the Hickory Dickory Doc!

There was a little girl, and she had a little curl
that drooped in the middle of her face.
To improve her view, she took some goo
and stuck it back in place.

Georgie Porgie, what a shame,
kids call you such a silly name.
Now I think you know it's true
that teasing isn't nice to do.

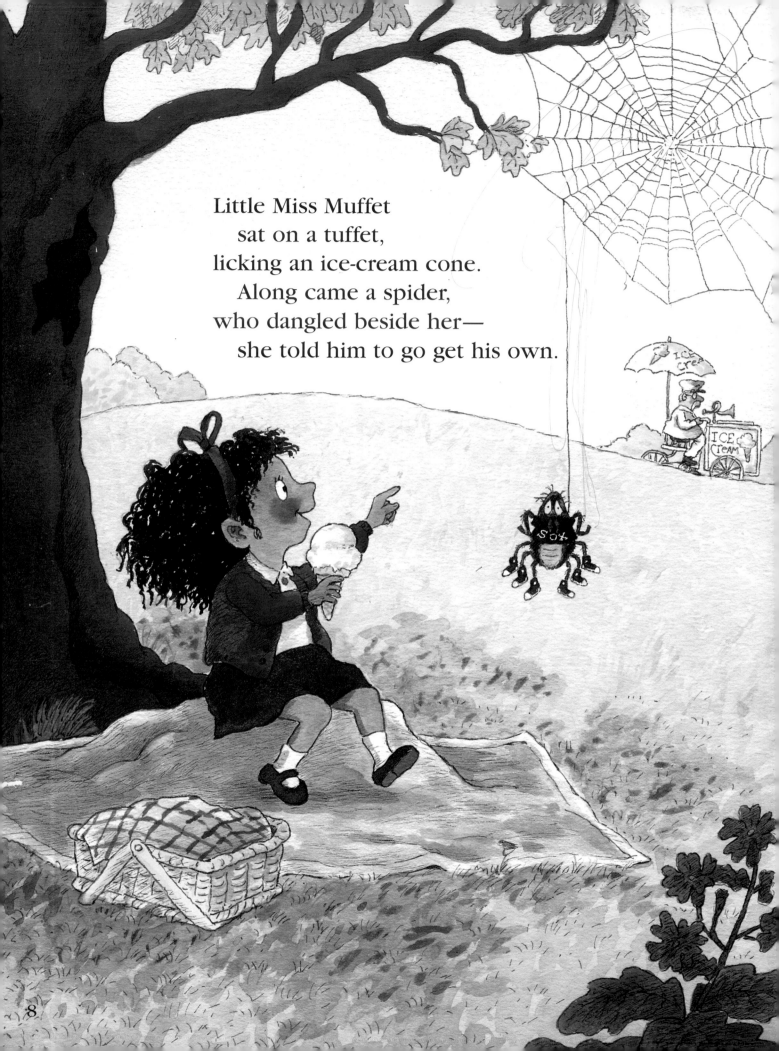

Little Miss Muffet
    sat on a tuffet,
licking an ice-cream cone.
    Along came a spider,
who dangled beside her—
    she told him to go get his own.

8

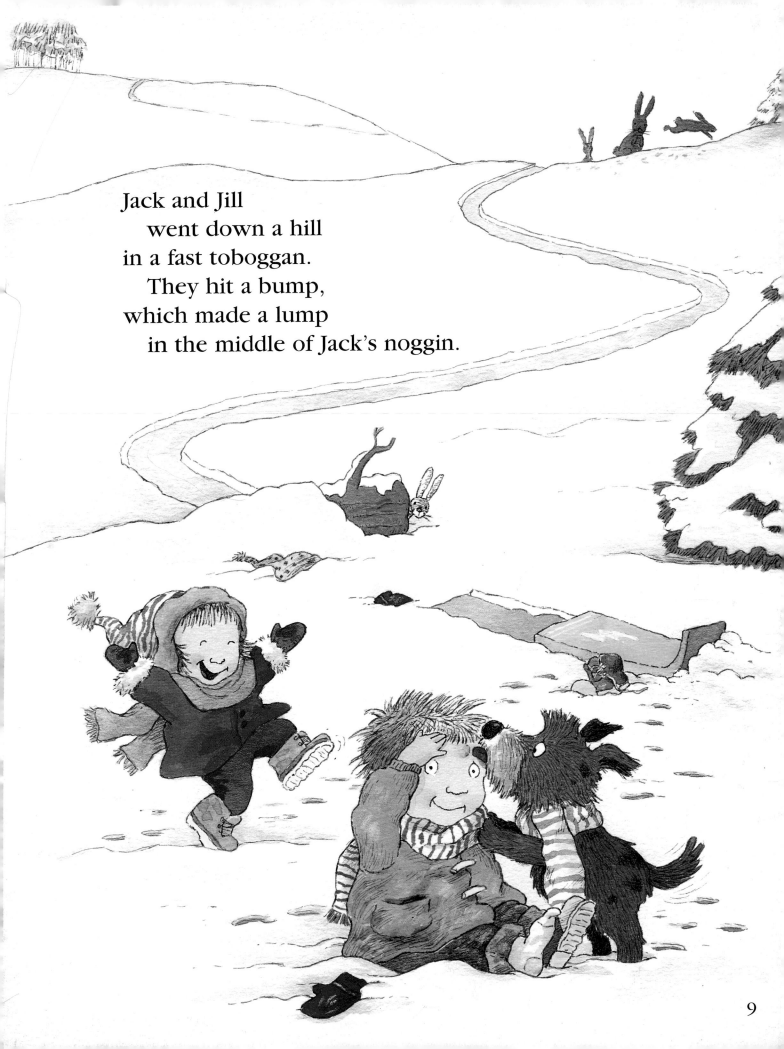

Jack and Jill
  went down a hill
in a fast toboggan.
  They hit a bump,
which made a lump
  in the middle of Jack's noggin.

9

Jack was nimble,
　Jack was quick.
Jack jumped over
　the candlestick.

Jack kept jumping,
　much too close.
Now his pants
　smell like burnt toast.

Little Bo-Peep throws her clothes in a heap,
which makes her room one giant mess.
And when she wakes up, she calls for her pup
to hunt through the heap for her dress.

Little Boy Blue,
    don't blow your horn.
You'll wake up the neighbors;
    it's two in the morn!
You've got to be quiet
    so people can sleep.
Get under your covers
    and try counting sheep.

Diddle diddle, dumpling, my girl June,
eats her lunch without a spoon.
She's a mess from head to toe—
so into the bathtub she must go.

Diddle diddle, dumpling, my son Scooter,
played around with my computer.
He pressed the buttons and hit the keys.
Now it only prints Chinese.

Row, row, row your boat,
gently 'round the lake.
Don't stand up and rock the boat—
that's a big mistake.

Rub-a-dub-dub,
    three men in a tub.
What do you think they said?
    "Too crowded, we fear,
let's get out of here,
    and each take a shower instead."

London Bridge is falling down,
    falling down, falling down.
There's no way to get to town.
    Take the ferry.

14

Humpty Dumpty sat on a wall.
 Humpty Dumpty had a great fall.
I wish they'd had super glue way back then—
 they could have put Humpty together again.

Mary, Mary, quite contrary,
what does your garden grow?
Spinach? Broccoli? Cauliflower?
To which Mary answered, "No!"

Tom, Tom, the teacher's son,
went to school when he was one.
The only thing young Tom could do
was play a game of peekaboo.

Old Mother Hubbard
    went to the cupboard
to get her poor dog a bone.
    But the dog couldn't wait,
so when dinner was late,
    he ordered a pizza by phone.

Peter, Peter, sugar eater,
    always wanted food much sweeter.
Adding sugar was a blunder.
    Now he is a toothless wonder.

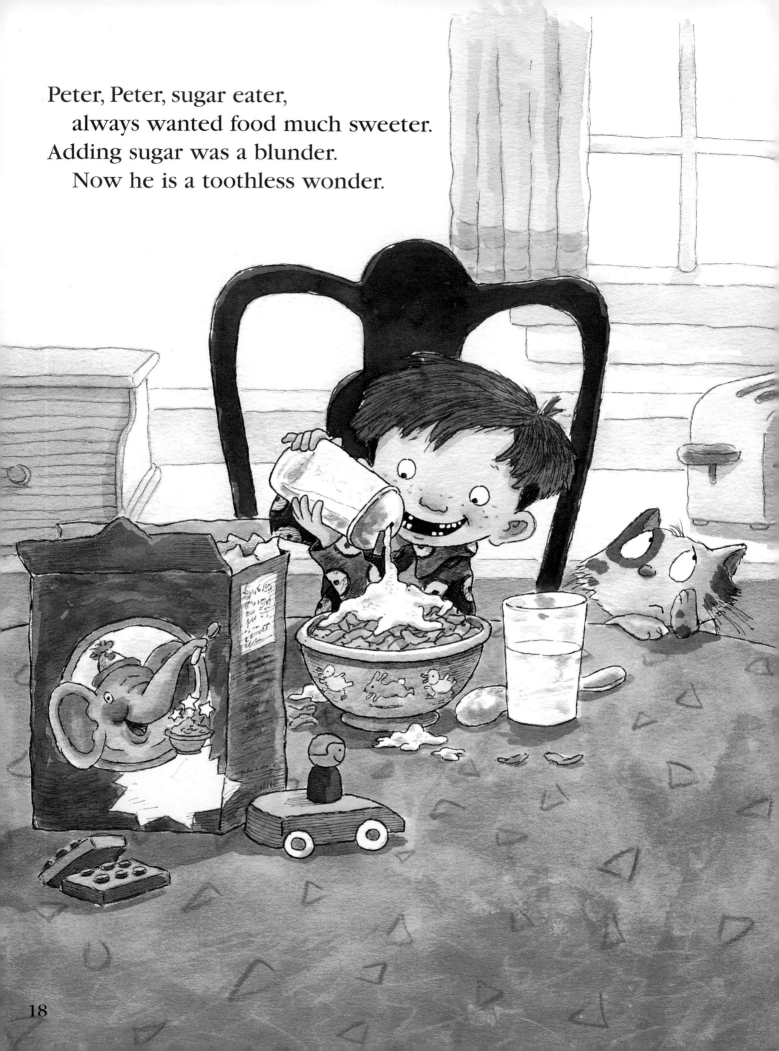

Violets are blue.
Roses are pink.
Please take a shower,
your feet really stink.

Hiccup, hiccup, go away!
Don't come back another day.

Some like it hot,
some like it cold,
but oatmeal tastes yucky
when it's nine days old.

Hey diddle, diddle,
   this rhyme is a riddle:
Can a cow fly over the moon?
   I bet you'll say, "No,"
but the answer is, "Yes" —
   if she's riding a hot-air balloon.

Lavender blue, rosemary green,
    when I am the king, you'll be the queen.
We'll sit on thrones, crowns on our heads.
    No one will send us up to our beds.

Old King Cole
        was a chubby old soul
who loved to play the fiddle.
    When given a chance,
    he'd often dance,
        till his pants split down the middle.

Pat a cake, pat a cake, baker Sue.
   Bake me a cake that says, "I love you."
I've saved up my money. I'm ready to pay.
   I'll give it to Mommy on Valentine's Day.

Pat a pie, pat a pie, baker Dan.
   Bake me a pizza as fast as you can.
Knead it, and roll it, and spread on the cheese.
   Then sprinkle on pepper; I'll try not to sneeze.

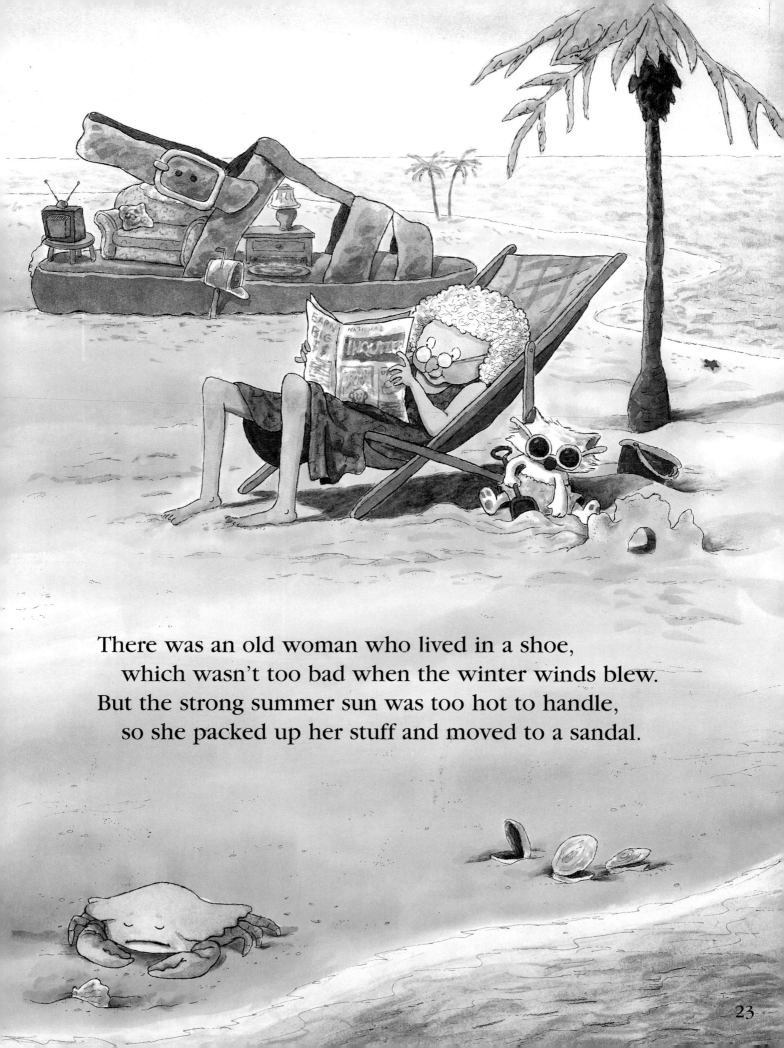

There was an old woman who lived in a shoe,
   which wasn't too bad when the winter winds blew.
But the strong summer sun was too hot to handle,
   so she packed up her stuff and moved to a sandal.

Mrs. Doodle went to town
riding on a gator.
She didn't feed the gator,
so the hungry gator ate 'er.

Yankee Doodle went to town
riding on a chicken.
He went into a restaurant
and came out finger lickin'.

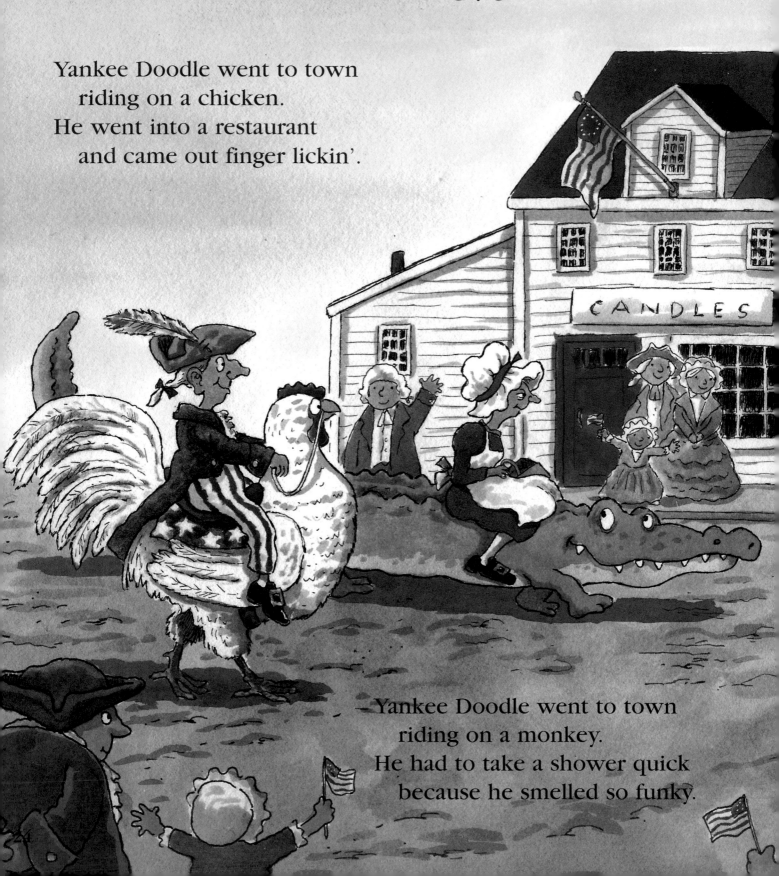

Yankee Doodle went to town
riding on a monkey.
He had to take a shower quick
because he smelled so funky.

Yankee Doodle went to town,
riding on a rooster.
His saddle wasn't high enough,
so now he's got a booster.

Jack Sprat would have no cat,
his wife would have no dog.
So when they went to buy a pet,
they settled on a frog.

Simple Simon met a snowman
standing with a broom.
"I'll give you fifty cents," he said,
"if you'll clean up my room."

Wee Willie Winkie ran down the stairs,
    hugging a blanket and two teddy bears.
"I can't fall asleep," he cried as he ran.
    "Look under my bed! There's a bogeyman!"

His father carried him up to his room.
    He turned on the light, then searched for a broom.
He swept some stuff from under the bed:
    two slippers, a bone, and Willie's dog, Fred.

I had a little pony,
   his name was Dapple-Gray.
I lent him to a woman,
   whose horse was sick one day.
But rain came down in showers
   and made puddles on the ground.
My pony got so muddy,
   I called him Dapple-Brown.

Three kind mice, see how they run!
   They all ran after the farmer's wife,
they took out some cheese,
   and they cut her a slice.
Did you ever see such a sight in your life
   as three kind mice?

Sweetheart, you're my little star.
How I love the way you are.
How I wonder what you'll be,
as I bounce you on my knee.

Twinkle, twinkle, little star.
How I wonder why you are
shining down on me so bright.
Please watch over me tonight.

Star light, star bright,
  first star I see tonight,
I'm going to try with all my might
  to keep my jammies dry all night.

31

Rock-a-bye, baby, on the treetop.
When the wind blows, the cradle will rock.
When the birds sing, the baby will smile,
and fall asleep happy in a short while.